THE
BUDDY BENCH

Written by **Patty Brozo**

Illustrated by **Mike Deas**

TILBURY HOUSE PUBLISHERS, THOMASTON, MAINE

"Class dismissed!" called Miss Mellon when the recess bell rang.

Her students ran out, one loud, happy gang.

They didn't waste time—recess was too short!

They started right in with their games and their sport.

Some boys climbed a mound,
playing king of the hill,
but though he stood near,
not one noticed Will.

Molly said to Brianne, "Let's play follow the leader."
They walked right by Emma but just didn't see her.

As Cooper watched
hide-and-seek from a tree,
he thought to himself,
Why does no one seek me?

Three kids played soldier
with a make-believe fort,
as Sloan looked on from the
basketball court.

Seven kids were clowns, and they acted quite silly.
They paraded right past, but no one saw Lily.

Jerome watched four kids playing blind man's bluff.

Why can't they see me? Aren't I big enough?

Three boys played with kites
that flew high in the air,
while Gabe sat and wondered,
Doesn't anyone care?

Then one dancing kite
dropped out of the sky,

and when Jake went to find it,
Gabe held it up high.

WHACK

"Want to join us," Jake asked, "before recess is done?
How come you're just watching? That can't be much fun."

"It's my leg," said Gabe. "I can't run in a cast,
so I never get picked, not even last."

"Come play with us anyway. There's time to spare."
"Wait a minute," said Gabe. "I'll be right there!"

Gabe hobbled to Will and tap-tapped his shoulder.
"Come and join us," he said, "before recess is over."

"I'm new here," said Will, "and today's my first day.
No one but you has asked me to play."

"Well, help us keep this kite in the air."
"Okay," said Will. "I'll be right there!"

Then Will went to Emma, and Emma to Sloan,
each asking the next why she was alone.

"There are holes in my pants and my shoes," Emma said.
"I don't fit in." And her face turned bright red.

"It's hard," said Sloan, "to know what to say.
I'm too scared to ask, but I do want to play."

"Come join us," said Will.
"There's no time to spare."
"Wait," said the girls.
"We'll be right there!"

They ran over to Cooper and said, "What about you?
We're gonna have fun. Can't you play too?"

"When I t . . . talk," explained Cooper, "my words get t . . . tangled.
What I want to s . . . say ends up all m . . . mangled."

"So what? Come and play," the two girls said.
"I'll come in a m . . . minute. You go on a . . . h . . . head!"

Then Cooper asked Lily, and Lily asked Jerome,
how come each of them was alone.

Lily told Cooper, "It's always the same.
I'm used to just watching. I'm no good at games."

"When you're small," said Jerome, "and the game is all tied, nobody wants you to be on their side."

"Come and p . . . play," Cooper said. "D . . . don't hang back and wait. Let's make some new friends. It's n . . . never too late."

But recess was over. The bell rang once more,
and Miss Mellon's students ran for the door.

"Miss Mellon," Will asked, "how could we say,
without using words, that we all want to play?
Sometimes we're too shy, too sad, or too proud.
How can we ask without asking out loud?"

bench

Miss Mellon said, "What you need is a seat
to wait for a friend or a buddy to meet."

"A *buddy bench!*" Miss Mellon's class all agreed.

"And we'll m . . . make it ourselves!" Cooper decreed.

So they borrowed a hammer,
a saw, and a wrench
and started to work
on their own special bench.

BANG! BANG! BANG! BANG!

When it was finished, they were all filled with pride.
Each child wore a smile that was nine inches wide.

"We think it's just perfect," the students all said,
"with hands that are colored blue, yellow, and red."

They put their new bench in the very best place—
under the climbing tree, right at its base.

Now everyone knows when they're feeling left out,
where to find friends, without any doubt.

And the words on the bench that they made on their own
say Buddy Bench = Nobody Alone.

ABOUT BUDDY BENCHES

Recess is supposed to be a fun break from the classroom, a chance to laugh and play, but a schoolyard can be a lonely place for a child on the sidelines.

The kids in this story share a few possible reasons for feeling left out, but there are more—almost as many more as there are children. In one study, 80% of 8- to 10-year-old kids reported feeling lonely at some point during a school day. Children's imaginations can make minor obstacles to inclusion seem insurmountable. Sometimes a friendly word or gesture is all that's needed to make an obstacle shrink or disappear.

That's why buddy benches—also known as friendship benches—are appearing in schoolyards around the world. When a child sits on the bench, it's a signal to other kids to ask him or her to play. The first buddy bench in the U.S. was the idea of Christian Bucks, a first-grader at Roundtown Elementary School in York, Pennsylvania, in 2013. Christian got the idea from Germany when he thought his family might be moving there, and the principal of Christian's school made it happen.

Buddy benches seem to work best when kids help to build them, but any bench or designated place in a schoolyard will work if kids understand the concept. Here are the rules that Christian's school came up with for their buddy bench:

- Before you sit on the bench, think of something you would like to do. Ask someone else to play with you.

- The bench isn't for socializing. Only sit there if you can't find anyone to play with.

- While you're sitting on the bench, look around for a game you can join.

- If you see something you want to do or a friend you want to talk to, get off the bench!

- When you see someone on the bench, ask that person to play with you.

- If you're sitting on the bench, play with the first classmate who invites you.

- Keep playing with your new friends!

Search on "buddy bench" online and you'll find a wealth of resources for further exploration. Here are a few:

Christian's Buddy Bench website:
www.buddybench.org

Cooper, Charlie, "How little people can make a big difference," 2014. In this TED Talk, a nine-year-old Australian boy describes how a buddy bench in his school reduced bullying.
https://www.youtube.com/watch?v=V7Z-Hq-xvxM

Groen, Sara K., "Buddy Bench: A Strategy to Increase Social Inclusion for Children with Special Needs." In partial fulfillment of a Master of Science in Curriculum and Instruction, St. Cloud State University, 2017.

Itkowitz, Colby, "Kids don't have to be lonely at recess anymore thanks to this little boy and his 'buddy bench,'" *Washington Post*, April 4, 2016.

Tilbury House Publishers
12 Starr Street
Thomaston, Maine 04861
www.tilburyhouse.com

Text © 2019 by Patty Brozo
Illustrations © 2019 by Mike Deas

Hardcover ISBN 978-0-88448-697-8
eBook ISBN 978-0-88448-699-2

First hardcover printing May 2019

15 16 17 18 19 20 XXX 10 9 8 7 6 5 4 3 2

Library of Congress Control Number: 2019901643

Designed by Frame25 Productions
Printed in China through Four Colour Print Group

PATTY BROZO has been writing stories for and about children since taking creative writing
classes in college. She is the author of *Miss Pinkeltink's Purse* (Tilbury House, 2018).

MIKE DEAS gets his flair for illustrative storytelling from an early love of reading and drawing. He fine-tuned his drawing skills and imagination at Capilano College's Commercial Ani-
mation Program in Vancouver, then worked as a concept artist, texture artist, and art lead
in the video game industry in England and California before returning to his native British
Columbia, Canada.